For Gabriella M.

British Library Cataloguing in Publication Data

McKee, David
  Snow woman
  I. Title
  823′.914 [J]   PZ7
ISBN 0-86264-103-9

First published in Great Britain by Andersen Press Ltd.,
62–65 Chandos Place, London WC2. Published in Australia by
Century Hutchinson Australia Pty. Ltd., 16–22 Church Street,
Hawthorn, Victoria 3122. All rights reserved. Colour
separated by Photolitho AG Offsetreproduktionen, Gossau,
Zürich, Switzerland. Printed in Italy by Grafiche AZ, Verona.

SNOW WOMAN

David McKee

Andersen Press · London
Century Hutchinson of Australia

"We're going to build a snowman," said Rupert.

"You mean a snowperson," said his father.

"We're going to build a snowman," said Rupert.

"You mean a snowperson," said his mother.

"I'm going to build a snow woman," said Kate.

"That's a good girl," said her mother.

"Snow woman? Nobody builds a snow woman," said
Rupert. "We'll build a snowman."

"You can build a snowman, I'm going to build a snow woman," said Kate.

Side by side they built their snowpeople.

Later they ran indoors again.

"I need a hat and scarf for the snowman," said Rupert.

"You mean snowperson," said his father.

"Can I have some clothes for the snow woman?" asked Kate.

"Certainly, dear," smiled Kate's mother.

They put the clothes on the snowpeople.

Then their mother took their photograph.

At bedtime, Rupert said, "Will the snowman be there in the morning?"

"You mean snowperson," said his father. "Yes, if it doesn't melt."

"Will the snow woman be there tomorrow?" asked Kate.

"I expect so, dear," said her mother.

"They've gone," gasped Rupert next morning.
"So have the clothes, so they didn't melt," said Kate.

"I've never heard of a snowman walking away before,"
said Rupert.

"Probably because he never had a snow woman
before," said Kate. "Now what shall we do?"

"Let's build a snow bear," said Rupert.
"Man bear or lady bear?" asked Kate.

"Just a bear," said Rupert.